MW00899151

THE RHYTHM NINJA

WRITTEN & ILLUSTRATED
BY MANDY L. BAILEY

No part of this book may be reproduced, stored in a retrievable system, or transmitted in any form or any means, electronic, mechanical, photocopying, recording, or otherwise, without written permission of the publisher.

Copyright © 2014 Mandy Lamm Bailey

ISBN-13: 978-0692242308 (Mandy Lamm Bailey)

ISBN-10: 0692242309

This book is dedicated to my precious husband, Jason, and our children, Julie-Anna and Coburn. They love and support me unconditionally, and join me in spontaneous outburst of music each and every day.

The Land of Rhythm was a simple land where happy Whole Notes lived. The well-rounded Whole Notes enjoyed doing their activities in groups of four. They ate four meals a day and their favorite meal was beets. In fact, each Whole Note ate four beets per day to help them keep their full, oval shape. The Whole Notes were one big happy family, living in perfect harmony.

Now each Whole Note in the land had a job. They all helped by taking turns doing the work to get each job done. Every Whole Note's favorite job was going to the farm to gather beets. This was always a fun adventure.

Farmer Forte's farm was the best place to get beets because he grew the tastiest beets around. He was loud and proud of his beets!

Farmer Forte sometimes hired a part-time helper when his beet sales were steady and strong. The helper's job was to cut the beets in half. This had never been an issue until he hired Rossini.

You see, Rossini was also known as Rossini the Rhythm Ninja. He wanted this job so that, during his free time, he could practice his ninja skills in the wide, open land.

Back in the Land of Rhythm, Haydn was the happiest Whole Note in town! He had been chosen to lead a group of Whole Notes to gather beets from Farmer Forte's farm. When all of the Whole Notes chosen for the trip arrived, they headed out to Farmer Forte's farm.

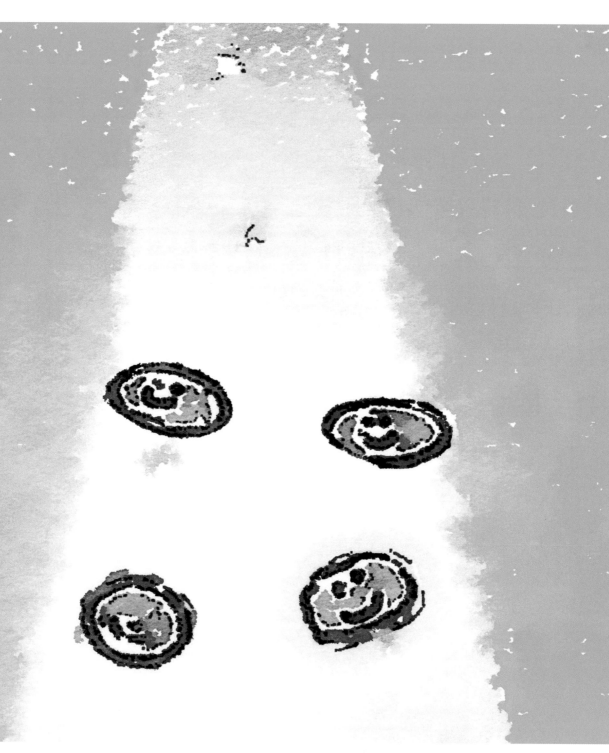

After a long journey, the Whole Notes were about to arrive at Farmer Forte's farm. Thinking he heard something strange, Haydn began to slow down. Suddenly, a crescendo of sound was heading right toward the Whole Notes. They caught a quick glimpse of something that appeared to be spinning round and round like a tornado. Too late, they realized they were in the path of the Rhythm Ninja!

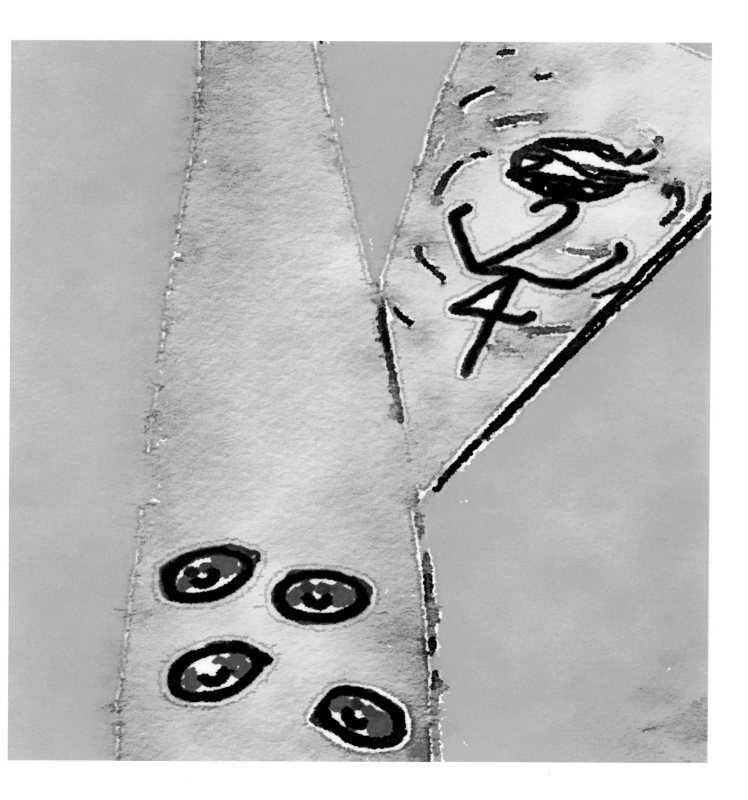

Rossini the Rhythm Ninja was spinning and slashing everything in sight. The Whole Notes weren't sure what had happened. One minute they were happily on their way to gather beets, and the next, they were all sprawled on the ground. Something was not quite right.

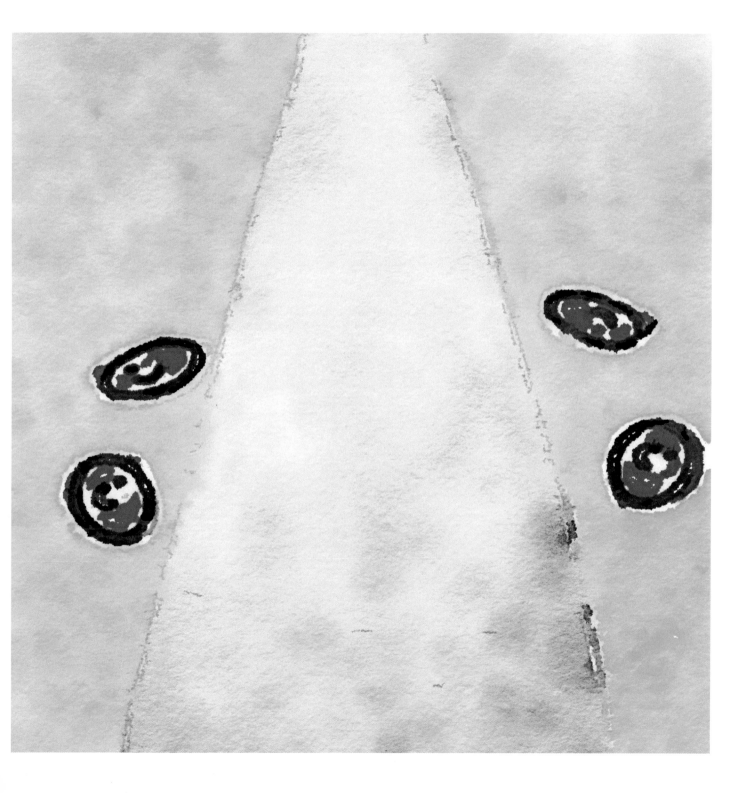

Back in the Land of Rhythm, Holly began to worry about Haydn and the other Whole Notes who had not returned. She heard on the Noteworthy News Station that there had been an accident near Farmer Forte's farm. She and some of her Whole Note friends decided to find the missing rhythms.

As they approached the farm, they found Haydn and their other friends lying on the roadside. Holly asked, "What happened to you? Are you all right?"

"I am not sure, but I think it was the Rhythm Ninja," Haydn answered. "We aren't hurt, but we are having a hard time moving around."

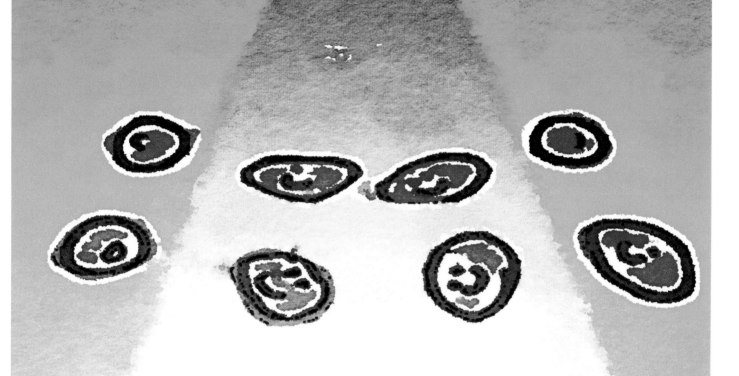

About that time, a music policeman, Treble Clef Trey, arrived on the scene. Treble Clef Trey began questioning Rossini the Rhythm Ninja.

"This was all an accident that happened while I was taking a break and practicing my ninja moves," Rossini explained. The Rhythm Ninja felt terrible. He apologized for the accident and asked how he could help.

Holly had a plan. She called the other Whole Notes together and said, "Let's gather walking sticks for Haydn and our Whole Note friends!"

Rossini the Rhythm Ninja and the Whole Notes went out in search of walking sticks. Holly found a field full of shrubs.

She gathered the stems from the shrubs and brought them to the injured Whole Notes. The stems were perfect! Haydn and all his friends were now able to get up and move with the help of the walking sticks. Some of them felt so good, they even walked on their heads!

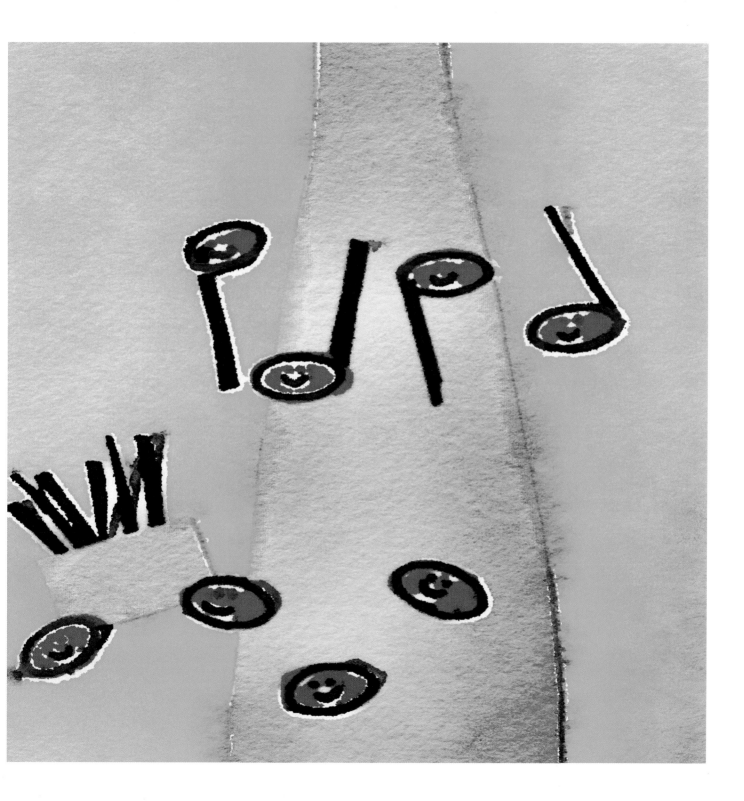

The walking sticks certainly gave them all a new look. They found their appetites had decreased, and they were only able to eat two beets each day. With only half of their appetites and a slimmer appearance, they became known as Half Notes.

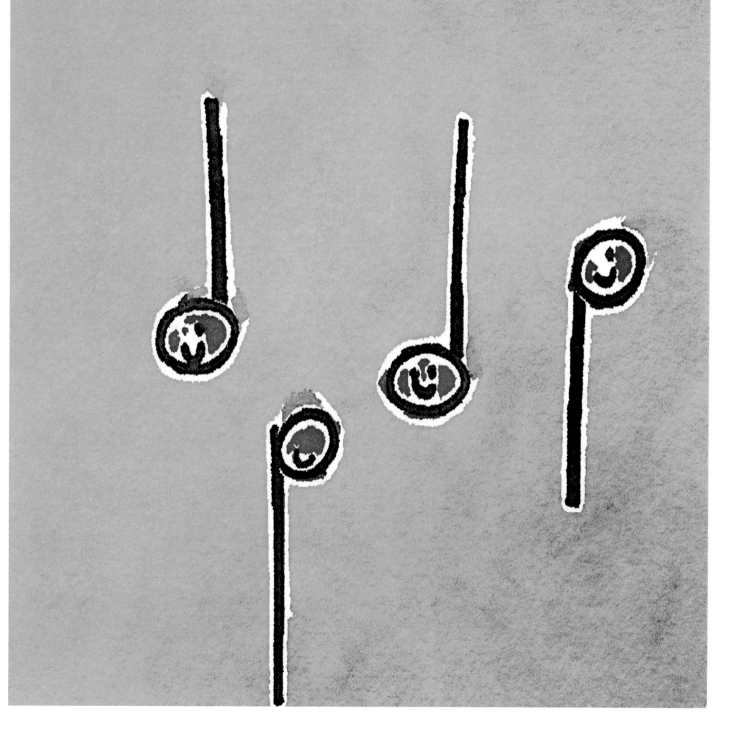

The time came when the Land of Rhythm needed more beets. After the last encounter with the Rhythm Ninja, the small group of Half Notes decided they should keep the job of going to gather beets. Feeling safe with their walking sticks, they traveled as a group to visit Farmer Forte's farm.

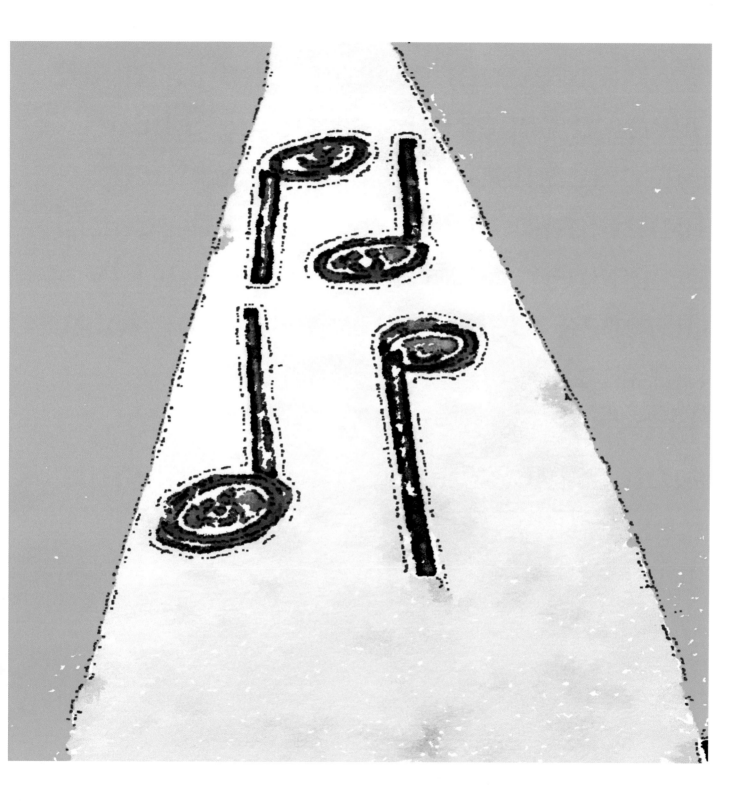

As they approached the farm, all seemed peaceful and quiet. Then, once again, out of nowhere, the familiar sound of a crescendo could be heard. The Half Notes quickly dropped to the ground, hoping to get out of the Rhythm Ninja's way. They also covered their faces to protect themselves, but once again, Rossini the Rhythm Ninja accidentally slashed every Half Note in sight.

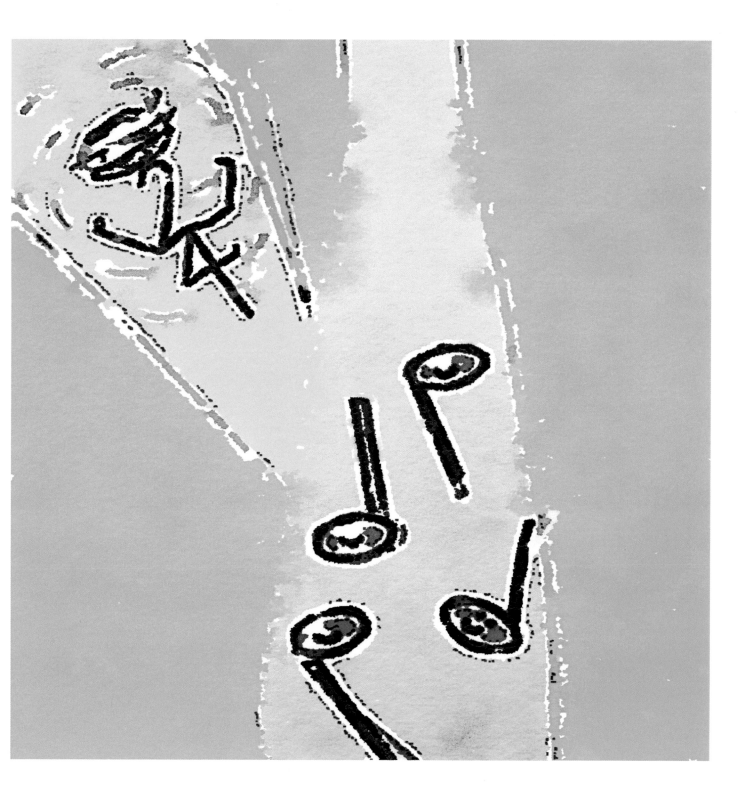

The Half Notes were not hurt. When Treble Clef Trey arrived on the scene to investigate, the Half Notes wouldn't show their faces. They felt safer with their faces covered, and they were embarrassed that they had been struck again by the Rhythm Ninja.

In many ways, the Half Notes looked the same, but their faces were now solid and covered. Also, they only required one beet per day. The Half Notes with covered faces became known as Quarter Notes.

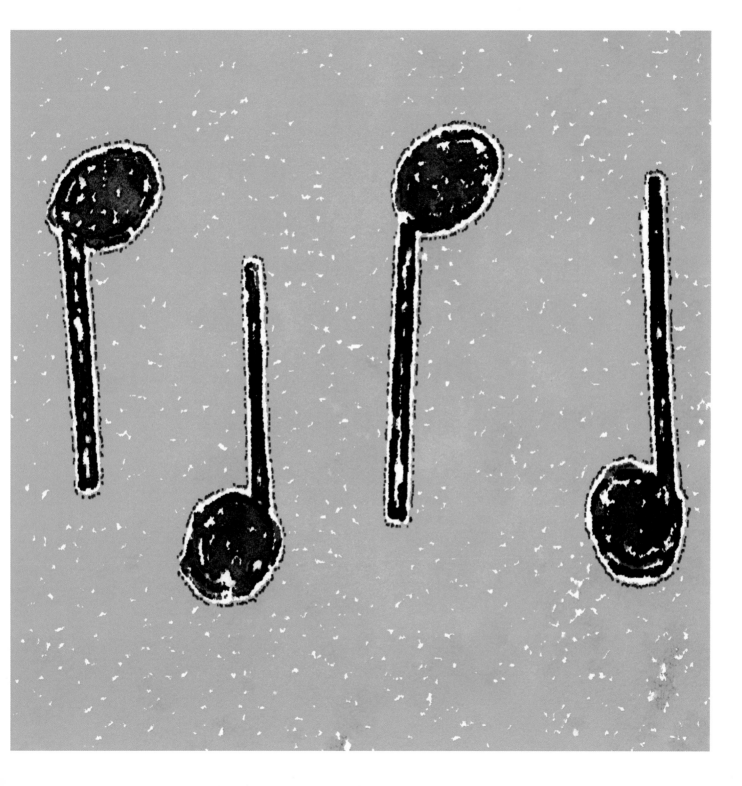

The next strike of the Rhythm Ninja occurred when the new Quarter Notes had the job of going to gather beets from Farmer Forte's farm. Thinking that the Rhythm Ninja could surely do no more harm, the Quarter Notes traveled as a group, unafraid. After all, they were armed with their walking sticks and their faces were forever covered.

Rossini the Rhythm Ninja was running late to work as he came spinning through town again. Since the faces of the Quarter Notes were covered, he only saw the walking sticks on the path.

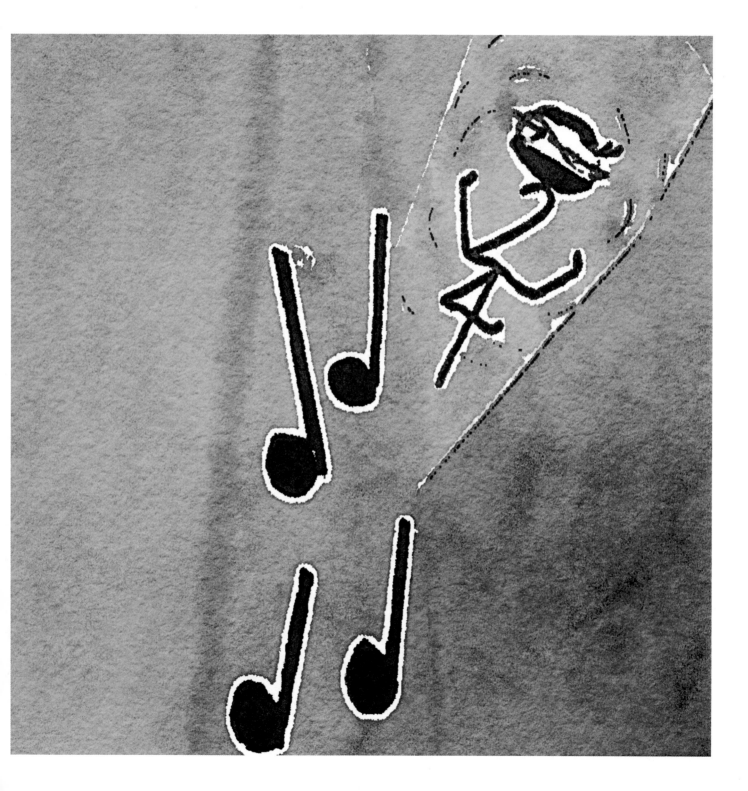

The Rhythm Ninja swiped the tops of the walking sticks, breaking the tips and leaving the stems at the top hanging on by a thread.

The Quarter Notes with broken tips were only able to eat half of a beet each day. They came to be called Eighth Notes.

The Rest of the Story

Finally the Land of Rhythm had enough of the Rhythm Ninja! They decided to have a staff meeting to discuss how to put a stop to his destructive ways. When the staff meeting took place, Farmer Forte was outraged. He became so loud, he was heard by the music police.

Treble Clef Trey and the music police force came and placed all of the Notes under arrest. The music police did not want any of this news to get out because it would scare others from visiting the Land of Rhythm. All of the rhythms at the meeting were silenced and ordered to never talk about the Rhythm Ninja.

Rossini the Rhythm Ninja agreed to move to the Land of Cut Time where cutting rhythms in half was allowed and encouraged.

The Whole Notes were now Whole Rests. They still ate four beets per day, but they were unable to speak. They began to hide behind upside-down hats. They carried their beets inside of their hats.

The Half Notes who were silenced hid inside of their upright hats. They continued eating only two beets per day, and were known as Half Rests. The Half Rests carried their beets on the brims of their hats.

The Quarter Notes were bent out of shape when told they couldn't speak. They continued to eat one beet per day and were known as Quarter Rests.

The Eighth Notes were so upset that they flipped out when they were silenced. They continued to eat only one half of a beet per day, in silence.

Coda

Rossini the Rhythm Ninja moved to the Land of Cut Time. Farmer Forte hired a full-time helper at the farm, and every note and rest lived in perfect harmony in the Land of Rhythm.

The End

Fine

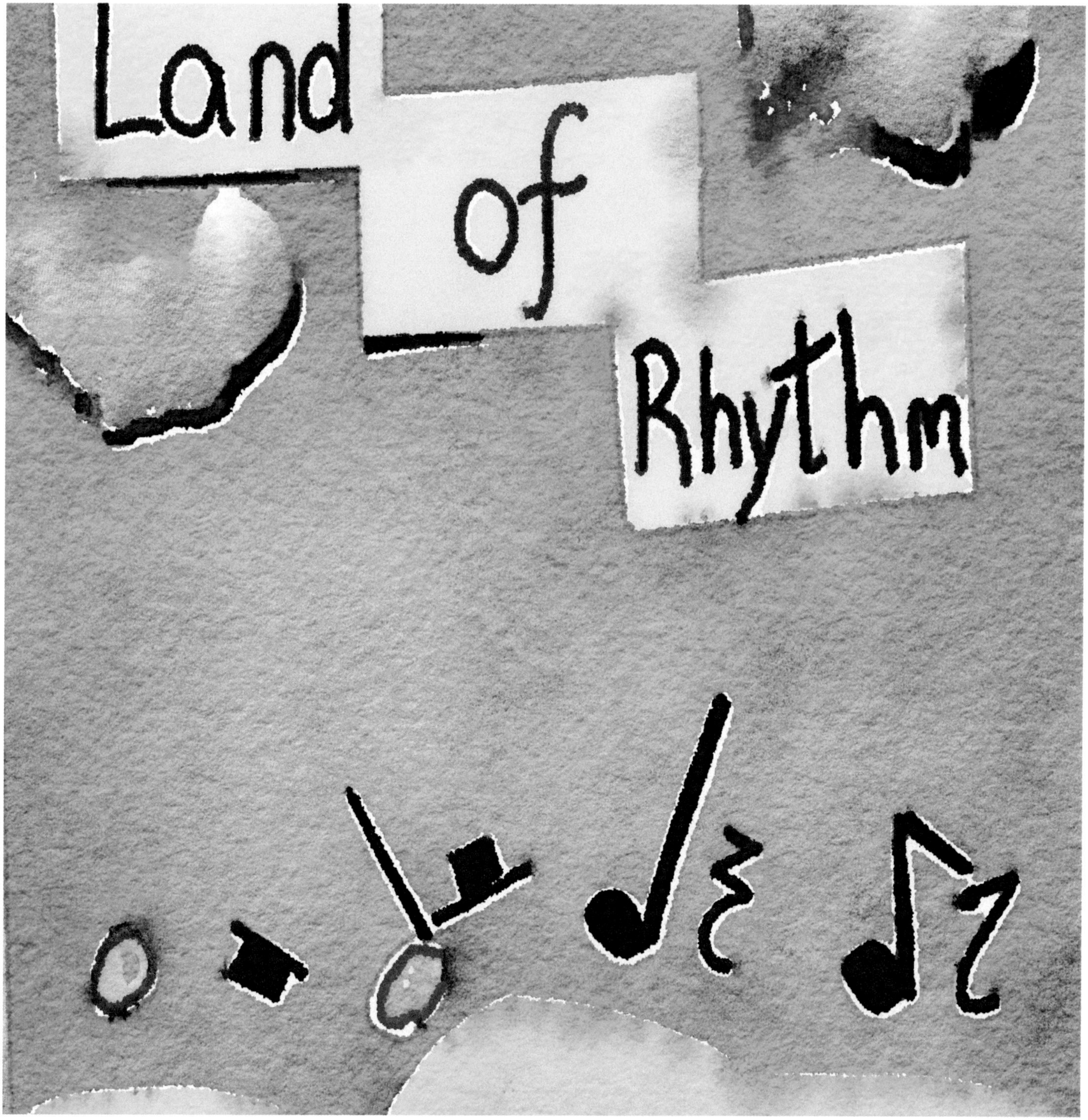
Land
of
Rhythm

Glossary

Coda – special ending in music

Crescendo – a gradual increase in dynamics (volume) in music

Eighth Note- a rhythmic value of ½ beat of sound

Eighth Rest- a rhythmic value of ½ beat of silence

Fine- word for "the end" in music

Forte- dynamic in music meaning loud

Half Note- rhythmic value for two beats of sound

Half Rest- rhythmic value for two beats of silence

Quarter Note- rhythmic value for one beat of sound

Quarter Rest- rhythmic value for one beat of silence

Staff- the five lines that musical pitches are written on in music

Treble Clef- symbol representing notes in a high range

Whole Note- rhythmic value of four beats of sound

Whole Rest- rhythmic value of four beats of silence

About The Author

Mandy Bailey lives in North Carolina with her husband and two children. While her music studies began as an instrumentalist, playing flute, she loved the possibilities and potential in shaping elementary students. After graduating from East Carolina University with a degree in Music Education, she began teaching general music in grades kindergarten through fifth grade. She has taught at Nashville Elementary school in Nashville, NC for sixteen years and is a National Board Certified Teacher in Early and Middle Childhood Music. Mandy has had several creative music teaching ideas and lessons published in national music educator magazines *MusicK8* and *Music Express.* She also serves in leadership roles on local and state levels creating music lessons and curriculum.

The Rhythm Ninja was created as she was teaching about rhythm values and animatedly showed her students how rhythms were slashed in half. Since the concept of the Rhythm Ninja has been such a successful teaching tool with her students (a population of over 700); she decided put her story to paper and share it. She hopes it will bring rhythms to life for other children. She believes what she learns from her own children helps her make connections with her students and uses relevant concepts to teach music in the most creative ways.

Made in the USA
Monee, IL
07 April 2022

94145638R00038